W9-API-269

WITHDRAWN

Ella May
DOES IT HER WAY!

For Oliver, Marlene and Frieda, with love. – A. S.

Quarto is the authority on a wide range of topics.

Quarto educates, entertains and enriches the lives of
our readers—enthusiasts and lovers of hands-on living.

www.quartoknows.com

© 2019 Quarto Publishing plc
Text © Mick Jackson
Illustrations © Andrea Stegmaier

Mick Jackson has asserted his right to be identified as the author of this work.
Andrea Stegmaier has asserted her right to be identified as the illustrator of this work.

First Published in 2019 by words & pictures,
an imprint of The Quarto Group.
6 Orchard Road, Suite 100, Lake Forest, CA 92630.
T: +1 949 380 7510
F: +1 949 380 7575
www.quartoknows.com

No part of this publication may be reproduced, stored in a retrieval system, or
transmitted in any form, or by any means, electrical, mechanical, photocopying,
recording or otherwise, without the prior written permission of the publisher
or a license permitting restricted copying. In the United Kingdom such licenses
are issued by the Copyright Licensing Agency, Barnard's Inn, 86 Fetter Lane,
London EC4A 1EN.

All rights reserved.

A CIP record for this book is available from the Library of Congress.

ISBN: 978 1 78603 905 7

9 8 7 6 5 4 3 2 1
Manufactured in Guangdong, China CC042019

VIGO COUNTY PUBLIC LIBRARY
TERRE HAUTE, INDIANA

MICK JACKSON   ANDREA STEGMAIER

Ella May
DOES IT HER WAY!

words & pictures

Say hello to Ella May.
A girl who does things her own way...

Likes dinosaurs

Likes insects
(but not beetles)

Likes stripes
(and apples)

This is her mom

This is her home

One day, Ella's mom gave
Ella something different to eat.
It looked, and smelled, *unusual*...

"Just try it," Ella's mom said.
"It's good to try new things."

Ella quite liked this idea.

So later
in the park,

Ella tried walking backward.
Just to see what it felt like.

It took a bit of getting used to.

Up in her bedroom, Ella tried reading a book backward. Which changed things quite a bit.

Then, after dinner, she went backward up to the bathroom.

And slept backward. Just to see how it felt.

The next day, Ella had lots
of backward adventures
on the playground.

This seemed to cause quite a stir with the other children.

Ella's mom hoped that sooner or later
Ella would get tired of walking backward.

But once Ella had set her mind on something...

...she liked to see it through.

So a few days later, when
Ella and her mom were
walking home from the store...

Ella's mom turned around and
walked backward next to Ella.
Just to see how it felt.

They passed the twins from down the road.
"That looks like fun," one said to the other.
"Can we try it?" they asked Ella.

They passed Mrs. Mercer...

...Graham's granddad...

...and Big Dave
and his dog.

They all wanted
to join in too.

Before long, a huge backward-walking
parade was marching through town.

But when they reached the bottom of the street
Ella stepped to one side and stopped.
She watched everyone walk away backward,
disappearing over the bridge.

"Is something wrong?" Ella's mom asked.
Ella thought for a minute.
"I think I'm done with walking backward," she said.

They set off again for home,
walking forward, side by side.

Ella's mom was secretly
relieved that Ella wasn't
walking backward anymore.

That is until...

Ella started doing cartwheels instead!
"Try it, Mom!" she said.
"It's good to try new things!"